BOOK REVIEWS

Here's what people are saying:

*The old circular-tale format
makes a neat device for working in
some reading reinforcement.*
from KIRKUS REVIEW

*The language is simple . . .
reassuring to hesitant readers.*
from SCHOOL LIBRARY JOURNAL

A warm, rhythmic story.
from BOOKLIST

Weekly Reader Books presents

LITTLE CHICK'S
STORY

by Mary DeBall Kwitz

Pictures by Cyndy Szekeres

An Early I CAN READ Book

Harper & Row, Publishers
New York, Hagerstown, San Francisco, London

This book is a presentation of Weekly Reader Books.
Weekly Reader Books offers book clubs for children
from preschool through high school. For further
information write to: **Weekly Reader Books,** 4343
Equity Drive, Columbus, Ohio 43228.

Published by arrangement with Harper & Row, Publishers, Inc.

Library of Congress Cataloging in Publication Data
Kwitz, Mary DeBall.
   Little Chick's story.

   (An Early I can read book)
   SUMMARY: Broody Hen tells Little Chick how she will
grow up and have chicks of her own some day.
   [1. Chickens—Fiction]   I. Szekeres, Cyndy.
II. Title.
PZ7.K976Li   [E]   77-11841
ISBN 0-06-023664-7
ISBN 0-06-023666-3 lib. bdg.

For my parents

Mary and Clark DeBall

Broody Hen laid five eggs.

She laid one egg in the hen house
for the farmer's son.

She laid one egg in the barn
for the farmer's daughter.

7

She laid one egg in the meadow

for the ring-tailed raccoon.

And she hid one egg

in the violets

for the Easter rabbit.

"One, two, three, four,"

counted Broody Hen.

Then she laid one more egg.

"This one is for me," she said.

And she fluffed out her feathers

and sat down on her egg.

She sat on it all day

in the sun.

She sat on it all night

in the dark.

She sat on her egg
when the wind blew
and when it rained.

And she clucked

a little hatching-out song.

"My chick-a-dee, my chick-a-dee,

my golden, downy chick-a-dee,

the sun is warm,

the wind blows free,

hatch out for me, my chick-a-dee."

15

And then one sunny, windy day
her egg hatched open.
And out came Little Chick.

16

Little Chick looked around her.

She looked up at Broody Hen.

"I'm hungry," said Little Chick.

"Eat, my chick-a-dee,"

said Broody Hen,

as she scratched up chicken feed.

Little Chick ran behind her,

pecking and eating,

until her stomach was full.

In the evening Little Chick

crept under Broody Hen's wing.

She peeked out at the dark

and the stars,

and said,

"Tell me a story, Broody Hen."

And Broody Hen did.

19

"Once upon a time," she said,
"there was a golden, downy
Little Chick.
She ate lots of chicken feed
and ran about in the sun
and the wind.

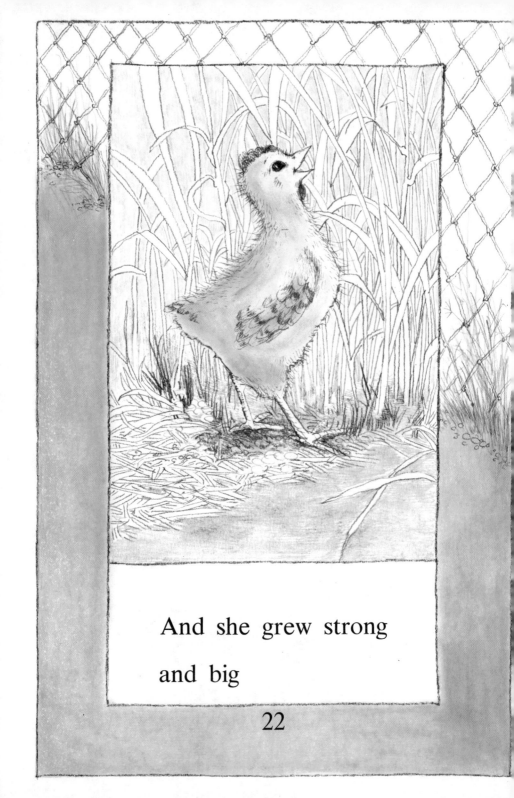

And she grew strong
and big

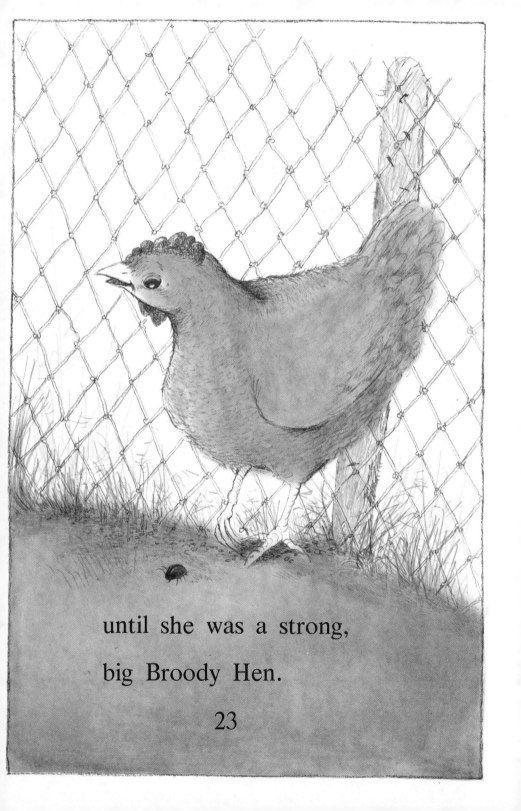

until she was a strong,

big Broody Hen.

23

Then she laid five eggs.

She laid one egg in the hen house
for the farmer's son.

She laid one egg in the barn
for the farmer's daughter.

She laid one egg in the meadow

for the ring-tailed raccoon.

And she hid one egg

in the violets

for the Easter rabbit.

27

Then that Little Chick,

grown strong and big

as a Broody Hen,

counted *One, two, three, four.*

And then she laid

one more egg...."

"Just for herself?"

asked Little Chick.

29

"Yes," said Broody Hen,

"just for herself."

Then Little Chick snuggled up
close to her mother.
And in the dark night,
under the stars,

Little Chick went to sleep.